This Little Tiger book belongs to:

_____

_____

_____

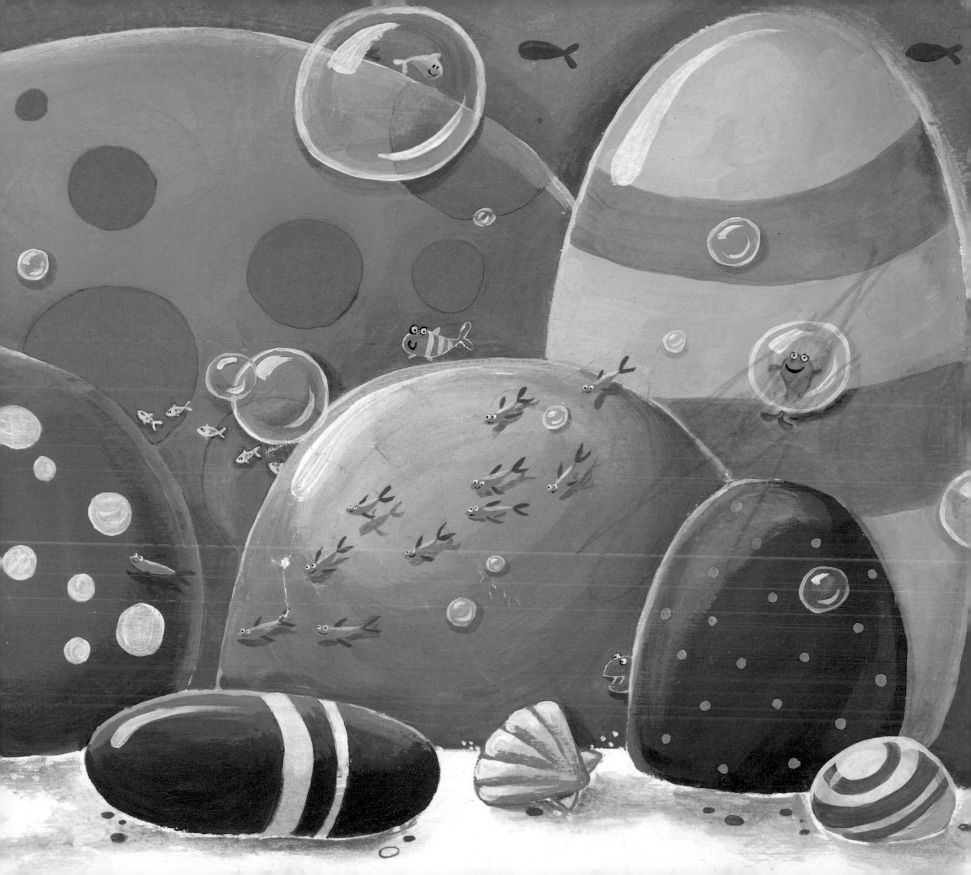

For Mortimer

This edition produced 2006 for
BOOKS ARE FUN LTD
1680 Hwy 1 North, Fairfield, Iowa, IA 52556
by LITTLE TIGER PRESS
An imprint of Magi Publications
1 The Coda Centre, 189 Munster Road, London SW6 6AW
www.littletigerpress.com
First published in Great Britain 2001
by Little Tiger Press, London
Text and illustrations copyright © Ruth Galloway 2001
ISBN-13: 978-1-84506-540-9
ISBN-10: 1-84506-540-9
Printed in China
1 3 5 7 9 10 8 6 4 2

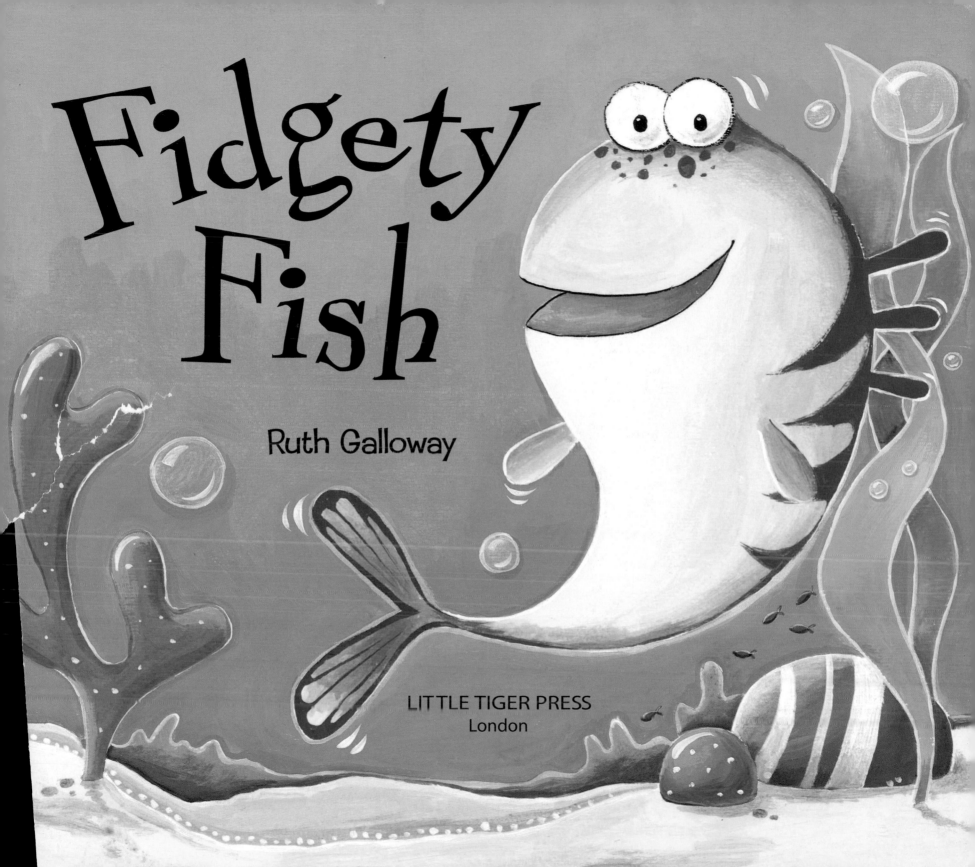

Fidgety Fish

Ruth Galloway

LITTLE TIGER PRESS

London

Tiddler was always fidgeting.

He wriggled and squiggled,

he darted and giggled . . .

until his mom got fed up with him.
"Go out into the sea and swim
till you're tired, but watch out for
the Big Fish," she said.
So Tiddler swam out of his cave.

He dived and he flipped,

he leapt and he dipped.

He sped faster than a rocket . . . .

and glided gently like a swan,
letting the sea currents fan his fins.

But he still didn't feel tired!

There were limpets that clung,

and jellyfish that stung.

Tiddler swam on towards
the big, red starfish . . .

and butted it gently with his nose.
The starfish just smiled, so . . .

Tiddler asked the clickety-clackety crab to play, but it scuttled off into the seaweed.

Tiddler came to a big, dark cave.
It looked much more exciting
than his cave back home,
and Tiddler swam in . . .

SNAP!

Tiddler was trapped inside the Big Fish!

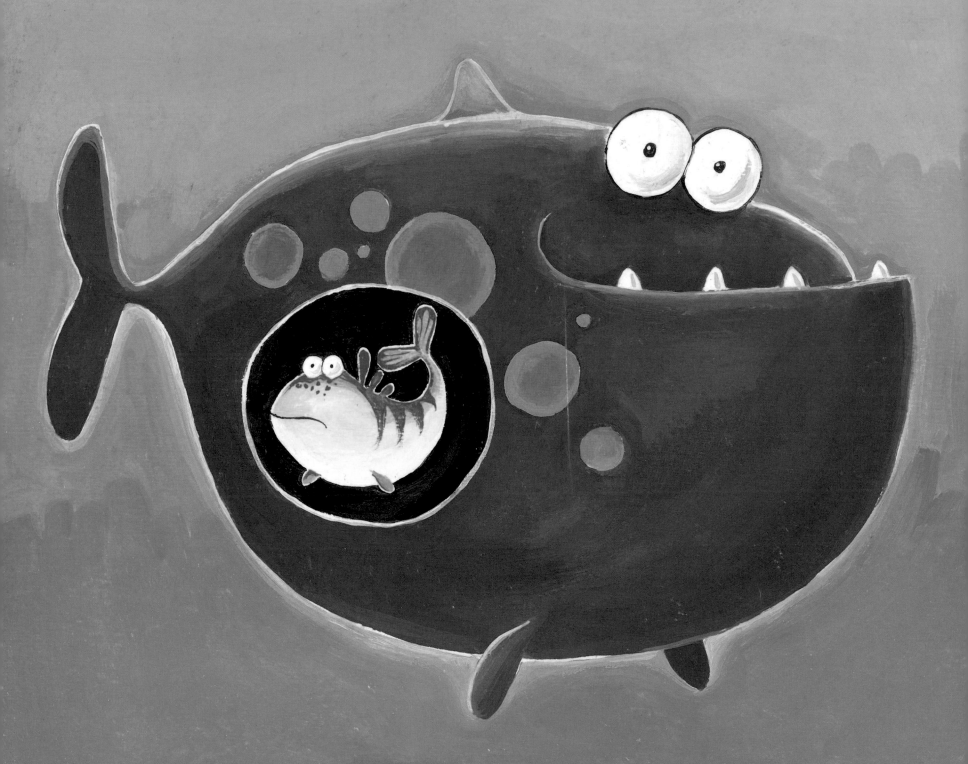

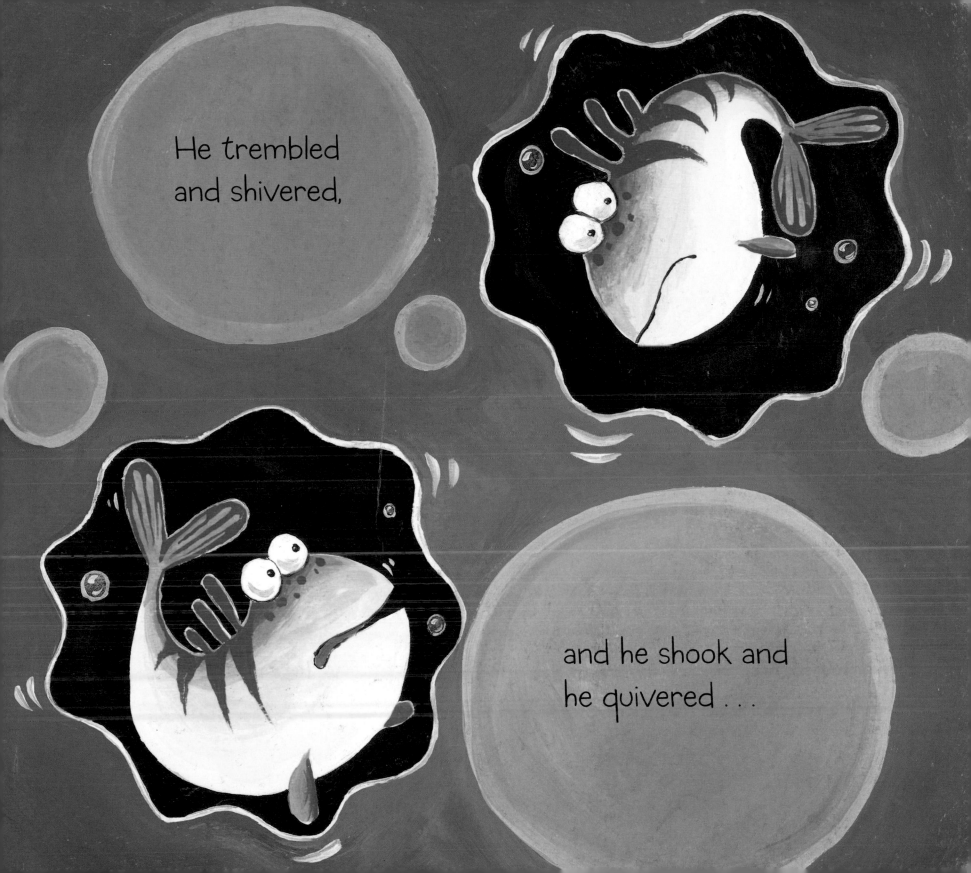

until the Big Fish's tummy began to feel very
funny indeed.

It rumbled and grumbled,
it turned and it tumbled.
It fluttered and groaned,
and mumbled and moaned.

Suddenly the Big Fish
did an enormous . . .

BURP!

And . . .

out shot Tiddler . . .

past the jellyfish,

and the clickety-clackety
crab hiding in the weeds,

past the starfish . . .

and straight through his own
front door!

"I hope you've used up all that
energy," said his mom . . .

but she would have to wait until the morning to hear about his adventures, because Tiddler was already fast asleep!